How the First letter was Written

Rudyard Kipling
Illustrated by Victor Ambrus

PETER BEDRICK BOOKS
NEW YORK

First American edition published in 1987 by Peter Bedrick Books 125 East 23 Street New York, NY 10010. Published by agreement with Macmillan Children's Books, a division of Macmillan Publishers Ltd., London & Basingstoke.

Text copyright The National Trust

Illustrations copyright © 1985 Macmillan Publishers Ltd.

Library of Congress Cataloging-in-Publication Data
    Kipling, Rudyard, 1865–1936.
        How the first letter was written.

        (A Just so story)
        Summary: When a cave man's spear breaks while fishing, his daughter composes the world's first letter and sends it home to her mother requesting the delivery of a new spear.
        [1. Letter writing—Fiction. 2. Cave dwellers—Fiction] I. Ambrus, Victor G., ill. II. Title. III. Series: Kipling, Rudyard, 1865–1936. Just so stories.
    PZ7.K632Hjc   1987   [E]   86–28886
    ISBN 0-87226-138-7 (lib. bdg.)

Printed in Hong Kong
Reinforced binding

ONCE upon a most early time was a Neolithic man. He was not a Jute or an Angle, or even a Dravidian, which he might well have been, Best Beloved, but never mind why. He was a Primitive, and he lived cavily in a Cave, and he wore very few clothes, and he couldn't read and he couldn't write and he didn't want to, and except when he was hungry he was quite happy. His name was Tegumai Bopsulai, and that means 'Man-who-does-not-put-his-foot-forward-in-a-hurry'; but we, O Best Beloved, will call him Tegumai, for short. And his wife's name was Teshumai Tewindrow, and that means 'Lady-who-asks-a-very-many-questions'; but we, O Best Beloved, will call her Teshumai, for short. And his little girl-daughter's name was Taffimai Metallumai, and that means 'Small-person-without-any-manners-who-ought-to-be-spanked'; but I'm going to call her Taffy. And she was Tegumai Bopsulai's Best Beloved and her own Mummy's Best Beloved, and she was not spanked half as much as was good for her; and they were all three very happy. As soon as Taffy could run about she went everywhere with her Daddy Tegumai, and sometimes they would not come home to the Cave till they were hungry, and then Teshumai Tewindrow would say, 'Where in the world have you two been to, to get so shocking dirty? Really, my Tegumai, you're no better than my Taffy.'

3

Now attend and listen!

One day Tegumai Bopsulai went down through the beaver-swamp to the Wagai river to spear carp-fish for dinner, and Taffy went too. Tegumai's spear was made of wood with shark's teeth at the end, and before he had caught any fish at all he accidentally broke it clean across by jabbing it down too hard on the bottom of the river. They were miles and miles from home (of course they had their lunch with them in a little bag), and Tegumai had forgotten to bring any extra spears.

'Here's a pretty kettle of fish!' said Tegumai. 'It will take me half the day to mend this.'

'There's your big black spear at home,' said Taffy. 'Let me run back to the Cave and ask Mummy to give it to me.'

'It's too far for your little fat legs,' said Tegumai. 'Besides, you might fall into the beaver-swamp and be drowned. We must make the best of a bad job.' He sat down and took out a little leather mendy-bag, full of reindeer-sinews and strips of leather, and lumps of beeswax and resin, and began to mend the spear. Taffy sat down too, with her toes in the water and her chin in her hand, and thought very hard. Then she said:–

'I say, Daddy, it's an awful nuisance that you and I don't know how to write, isn't it? If we did we could send a message for the new spear.'

'Taffy,' said Tegumai, 'how often have I told you not to use slang? "Awful" isn't a pretty word, – but it *would* be a convenience, now you mention it, if we could write home.'

Just then a Stranger-man came along the river, but he belonged to a far tribe, the Tewaras, and he did not understand one word of Tegumai's language. He stood on the bank and smiled at Taffy, because he had a little girl-daughter of his own at home. Tegumai drew a hank of deer-sinews from his mendy-bag and began to mend his spear.

'Come here,' said Taffy. 'Do you know where my Mummy lives?' And the Stranger-man said 'Um!' – being, as you know, a Tewara.

'Silly!' said Taffy, and she stamped her foot, because she saw a shoal of very big carp going up the river just when her Daddy couldn't use his spear.

'Don't bother grown-ups,' said Tegumai, so busy with his spear-mending that he did not turn round.

'I aren't,' said Taffy. 'I only want him to do what I want him to do, and he won't understand.'

'Then don't bother me,' said Tegumai, and he went on pulling and straining at the deer-sinews with his mouth full of loose ends. The Stranger-man – a genuine Tewara he was – sat down on the grass, and Taffy showed him what her Daddy was doing. The Stranger-man thought, 'This is a very wonderful child. She stamps her foot at me and she makes faces. She must be the daughter of that noble Chief who is so great that he won't take any notice of me.' So he smiled more politely than ever.

'Now,' said Taffy, 'I want you to go to my Mummy, because your legs are longer than mine, and you won't fall into the beaver-swamp, and ask for Daddy's other spear – the one with the black handle that hangs over our fireplace.'

The Stranger-man (*and* he was a Tewara) thought, 'This is a very, very wonderful child. She waves her arms and she shouts at me, but I don't understand a word of what she says. But if I don't do what she wants, I greatly fear that that haughty Chief, Man-who-turns-his-back-on-callers, will be angry.' He got up and twisted a big flat piece of bark off a birch-tree and gave it to Taffy. He did this, Best Beloved, to show that his heart was as white as the birch-bark and that he meant no harm; but Taffy didn't quite understand.

'Oh!' said she. 'Now I see! You want my Mummy's living-address? Of course I can't write, but I can draw pictures if I've anything sharp to scratch with. Please lend me the shark's tooth off your necklace.'

The Stranger-man (and *he* was a Tewara) didn't say anything, so Taffy put up her little hand and pulled at the beautiful bead and seed and shark-tooth necklace round his neck.

The Stranger-man (and he *was* a Tewara) thought, 'This is a very, very wonderful child. The shark's tooth on my necklace is a magic shark's tooth, and I was always told that if anybody touched it without my leave they would immediately swell up or burst. But this child doesn't swell up or burst, and that important Chief, Man-who-attends-strictly-to-his-business, who has not yet taken any notice of me at all, doesn't seem to be afraid that she will swell up or burst. I had better be more polite.'

So he gave Taffy the shark's tooth, and she lay down flat on her tummy with her legs in the air, like some people on the drawing-room floor when they want to draw pictures, and she said, 'Now I'll draw you some beautiful pictures! You can look over my shoulder, but you mustn't joggle. First I'll draw Daddy fishing. It isn't very like him; but Mummy will know, because I've drawn his spear all broken. Well, now I'll draw the other spear that he wants, the black-handled spear. It looks as if it was sticking in Daddy's back, but that's because the shark's tooth slipped and this piece of bark isn't big enough. That's the spear I want you to fetch; so I'll draw a picture of me myself 'splaining to you. My hair doesn't stand up like I've drawn, but it's easier to draw that way. Now I'll draw you. *I* think you're very nice really, but I can't make you pretty in the picture, so you mustn't be 'fended. Are you 'fended?'

The Stranger-man (and he was *a* Tewara) smiled. He thought, 'There must be a big battle going to be fought somewhere, and this extraordinary child, who takes my magic shark's tooth but who does not swell up or burst, is telling me to call all the great Chief's tribe to help him. He *is* a great Chief, or he would have noticed me.'

'Look,' said Taffy, drawing very hard and rather scratchily, 'now I've drawn you, and I've put the spear that Daddy wants into your hand, just to remind you that you're to bring it. Now I'll show you how to find my Mummy's living-address. You go along till you come to two trees (those are trees), and then you go over a hill (that's a hill), and then you come into a beaver-swamp all full of beavers. I haven't put in all the beavers, because I can't draw beavers, but I've drawn their heads, and that's all you'll see of them when you cross the swamp. Mind you don't fall in! Then our Cave is just beyond the beaver-swamp. It isn't as high as the hills really, but I can't draw things very small. That's my Mummy outside. She is beautiful. She is the most beautifullest Mummy there ever was, but she won't be 'fended when she sees I've drawn her so plain. She'll be pleased of me because I can draw. Now, in case you forget, I've drawn the spear that Daddy wants *outside* our Cave. It's *inside* really, but you show the picture to my Mummy and she'll give it you. I've made her holding up her hands, because I know she'll be so pleased to see you. Isn't it a beautiful picture? And do you quite understand, or shall I 'splain again?'

The Stranger-man (and he was a *Tewara*) looked at the picture and nodded very hard. He said to himself, 'If I do not fetch this great Chief's tribe to help him, he will be slain by his enemies who are coming up on all sides with spears. Now I see why the great Chief pretended not to notice me! He feared that his enemies were hiding in the bushes and would see him deliver a message to me. Therefore he turned his back, and let the wise and wonderful child draw the terrible picture showing me his difficulties. I will away and get help for him from his tribe.' He did not even ask Taffy the road, but raced off into the bushes like the wind, with the birch-bark in his hand, and Taffy sat down most pleased.

Now this is the picture that Taffy had drawn for him!

'What have you been doing, Taffy?' said Tegumai. He had mended his spear and was carefully waving it to and fro.

'It's a little berangement of my own, Daddy dear,' said Taffy. 'If you won't ask me questions, you'll know all about it in a little time, and you'll be surprised. You don't know how surprised you'll be, Daddy! Promise you'll be surprised.'

'Very well,' said Tegumai, and went on fishing.

The Stranger-man – did you know he was a Tewara? – hurried away with the picture and ran for some miles, till quite by accident he found Teshumai Tewindrow at the door of her Cave, talking to some other Neolithic ladies who had come in to a Primitive lunch. Taffy was very like Teshumai, specially about the upper part of the face and the eyes, so the Stranger-man – always a pure Tewara – smiled politely and handed Teshumai the birch-bark. He had run hard, so that he panted, and his legs were scratched with brambles, but he still tried to be polite.

As soon as Teshumai saw the picture she screamed like anything and flew at the Stranger-man. The other Neolithic ladies at once knocked him down and sat on him in a long line of six, while Teshumai pulled his hair. 'It's as plain as the nose on this Stranger-man's face,' she said. 'He has stuck my Tegumai all full of spears, and frightened poor Taffy so that her hair stands all on end; and not content with that, he brings me a horrid picture of how it was done. Look!' She showed the picture to all the Neolithic ladies sitting patiently on the Stranger-man. 'Here is my Tegumai with his arm broken; here is a spear sticking into his back; here is a man with a spear ready to throw; here is another man throwing a spear from a Cave, and here are a whole pack of people' (they were Taffy's beavers really, but they did look rather like people) 'coming up behind Tegumai. Isn't it shocking!'

15

'Most shocking!' said the Neolithic ladies, and they filled the Stranger-man's hair with mud (at which he was surprised), and they beat upon the Reverberating Tribal Drums, and called together all the Chiefs of the Tribe of Tegumai, with their Hetmans and Dolmans, all Neguses, Woons, and Akhoonds of the organisation, in addition to the Warlocks, Angekoks, Jujumen, Bonzes, and the rest, who decided that before they chopped the Stranger-man's head off he should instantly lead them down to the river and show them where he had hidden poor Taffy.

By this time the Stranger-man (in spite of being a Tewara) was really annoyed. They had filled his hair quite solid with mud; they had rolled him up and down on knobbly pebbles; they had sat upon him in a long line of six; they had thumped him and bumped him until he could hardly breathe; and though he did not understand their language, he was almost sure that the names the Neolithic ladies called him were not ladylike. However, he said nothing till all the Tribe of Tegumai were assembled, and then he led them back to the bank of the Wagai river, and there they found Taffy making daisy-chains, and Tegumai carefully spearing small carp with his mended spear.

'Well, you *have* been quick!' said Taffy. 'But why did you bring so many people? Daddy, dear, this is my surprise. *Are* you surprised, Daddy?'

'Very,' said Tegumai; 'but it has ruined all my fishing for the day. Why, the whole dear, kind, nice, clean, quiet Tribe is here, Taffy.'

And so they were. First of all walked Teshumai Tewindrow and the Neolithic ladies, tightly holding on to the Stranger-man, whose hair was full of mud (although he was a Tewara). Behind them came the Head Chief, the Vice-Chief, the Deputy and Assistant Chiefs (all armed to the upper teeth), the Hetmans and Heads of Hundreds, Platoffs with their Platoons, and Dolmans with their Detachments; Woons, Neguses, and Akhoonds ranking in the rear (still armed to the teeth). Behind them was the Tribe in hierarchical order, from owners of four caves (one for each season), a private reindeer-run, and two salmon-leaps, to feudal and prognathous Villeins, semi-entitled to half a bearskin of winter nights, seven yards from the fire, and adscript serfs, holding the reversion of a scraped marrow-bone under heriot (Aren't those beautiful words, Best Beloved?). They were all there, prancing and shouting, and they frightened every fish for twenty miles, and Tegumai thanked them in a fluid Neolithic oration.

Then Teshumai Tewindrow ran down and kissed and hugged Taffy very much indeed; but the Head Chief of the Tribe of Tegumai took Tegumai by the top-knot feathers and shook him severely.

'Explain! Explain! Explain!' cried all the Tribe of Tegumai.

'Goodness' sakes alive!' said Tegumai. 'Let go of my top-knot. Can't a man break his carp-spear without the whole countryside descending on him? You're a very interfering people.'

'I don't believe you've brought my Daddy's black-handled spear after all,' said Taffy. 'And what *are* you doing to my nice Stranger-man?'

They were thumping him by twos and threes and tens till his eyes turned round and round. He could only gasp and point at Taffy.

'Where are the bad people who speared you, my darling?' said Teshumai Tewindrow.

'There weren't any,' said Tegumai. 'My only visitor this morning was the poor fellow that you are trying to choke. Aren't you well, or are you ill, O Tribe of Tegumai?'

'He came with a horrible picture,' said the Head Chief, – 'a picture that showed you were full of spears.'

'Er – um – P'raps I'd better 'splain that I gave him that picture,' said Taffy, but she did not feel quite comfy.

'You!' said the Tribe of Tegumai all together. 'Small-person-with-no-manners-who-ought-to-be-spanked! You?'

'Taffy, dear, I'm afraid we're in for a little trouble,' said her Daddy, and put his arm round her, so she didn't care.

'Explain! Explain! Explain!' said the Head Chief of the Tribe of Tegumai, and he hopped on one foot.

'I wanted the Stranger-man to fetch Daddy's spear, so I drawded it,' said Taffy. 'There wasn't lots of spears. There was only one spear. I drawded it three times to make sure. I couldn't help it looking as if it stuck into Daddy's head – there wasn't room on the birch-bark; and those things that Mummy called bad people are my beavers. I drawded them to show him the way through the swamp; and I drawded Mummy at the mouth of the Cave looking pleased because he is a nice Stranger-man, and *I* think you are just the stupidest people in the world,' said Taffy. 'He is a very nice man. Why have you filled his hair with mud? Wash him!'

Nobody said anything at all for a long time, till the Head Chief laughed; then the Stranger-man (who was at least a Tewara) laughed; then Tegumai laughed till he fell down flat on the bank; then all the Tribe laughed more and worse and louder. The only people who did not laugh were Teshumai Tewindrow and all the Neolithic ladies. They were very polite to all their husbands, and said 'Idiot!' ever so often.

Then the Head Chief of the Tribe of Tegumai cried and
said and sang, 'O Small-person-without-any-manners-who-
ought-to-be-spanked, you've hit upon a great invention!'

'I didn't intend to; I only wanted Daddy's black-handled
spear,' said Taffy.

'Never mind. It *is* a great invention, and some day men will call it writing. At present it is only pictures, and, as we have seen to-day, pictures are not always properly understood. But a time will come, O Babe of Tegumai, when we shall make letters – all twenty-six of 'em, – and when we shall be able to read as well as to write, and then we shall always say exactly what we mean without any mistakes. Let the Neolithic ladies wash the mud out of the stranger's hair!'

'I shall be glad of that,' said Taffy, 'because, after all, though you've brought every single other spear in the Tribe of Tegumai, you've forgotten my daddy's black-handled spear.'

Then the Head Chief cried and said and sang, 'Taffy, dear, the next time you write a picture-letter, you'd better send a man who can talk our language with it, to explain what it means. I don't mind it myself, because I am a Head Chief, but it's very bad for the rest of the Tribe of Tegumai, and, as you can see, it surprises the stranger.'

Then they adopted the Stranger-man (a genuine Tewara of Tewar) into the Tribe of Tegumai, because he was a gentleman and did not make a fuss about the mud that the Neolithic ladies had put into his hair. But from that day to this (and I suppose it is all Taffy's fault), very few little girls have ever liked learning to read or write. Most of them prefer to draw pictures and play about with their Daddies – just like Taffy.

There runs a road by Merrow Down –
    A grassy track to-day it is –
An hour out of Guildford town,
    Above the river Wey it is.

Here, when they heard the horse-bells ring,
    The ancient Britons dressed and rode
To watch the dark Phoenicians bring
    Their goods along the Western Road.

And here, or hereabouts, they met
    To hold their racial talks and such –
To barter beads for Whitby jet,
    And tin for gay shell torques and such.

But long and long before that time
    (When bison used to roam on it)
Did Taffy and her Daddy climb
    That down, and had their home on it.

Then beavers built in Broadstonebrook
    And made a swamp where Bramley stands;
And bears from Shere would come and look
    For Taffimai where Shamley stands.

The Wey, that Taffy called Wagai,
    Was more than six times bigger then;
And all the Tribe of Tegumai
    They cut a noble figure then!